Happy Reading!

Snip Francis

Melanie
Gilbert

Hey Look!
The Happy Book

Published in the United States of America
by Little Salamander Press
Penobscot Building
645 Griswold
P.O. Box 310759
Detroit, MI 48231

www.littlesalamander.com

Francis, Snip/Gilbert, Melanie
Hey Look! The Happy Book.
Text and illustrations by Snip Francis and Melanie Gilbert;
Editor Lisa Johanna Gilbert and Susan Reames

Summary: This charming picture book of rhyming text celebrates all of
the beauty in the world; from the stars in the sky to the fishes in
the ocean. The story lovingly affirms each child's special place in the world.

ISBN: 1-890616-22-2
1. Bedtime – fiction. 2. Imagination – fiction. 3. Story in rhyme.
Library of Congress Catalog Number 97-074671

Book cover and design by Inari, Inc.
Printed in Canada by Friesens
10 9 8 7 6 5 4 3 2

To my parents, Ellen and George Francis,
who truly mean the world to me.

To my parents, Johanna and Ellwyn Gilbert.
Je vous aime beaucoup, cheris

To Poohbala.
Happy, happy, happy, is what you make me, me, me.

A little story
for you.

Of all the stars in the sky

and the planets that glow,

Of all the mountains on high

and the dragons below,

Of all the creatures that play

on the land and in air,

Of all the children who pray

for a dream, hope, or care,

Of all the snowflakes that fall

and the snowmen they bring,

Of all the bugs big and small

who can crawl, fly, and sing,

Of all the fishes that swim

in the blue, shining sea,

Only you, only you . . .

mean the world to me.

The End.

Instructions for the Happy Puppets

You can create your own *Hey Look! The Happy Book* story, too.

Just cut out the puppets that are included in the back of this book.

Make up your own story and invite people to your puppet show. Use the back of a couch or the inside of a cut out box as your puppet theater.

Play with the puppets by yourself or with a friend.

Have fun sharing your happy stories with all the people in your world!

Remember: Scissors are not toys and should always be used with adult supervision.

If you would like an additional or a replacement set of puppets, please send $3.50 to:
Little Salamander Press
Penobscot Building
P.O. Box 310759
Detroit, MI 48231